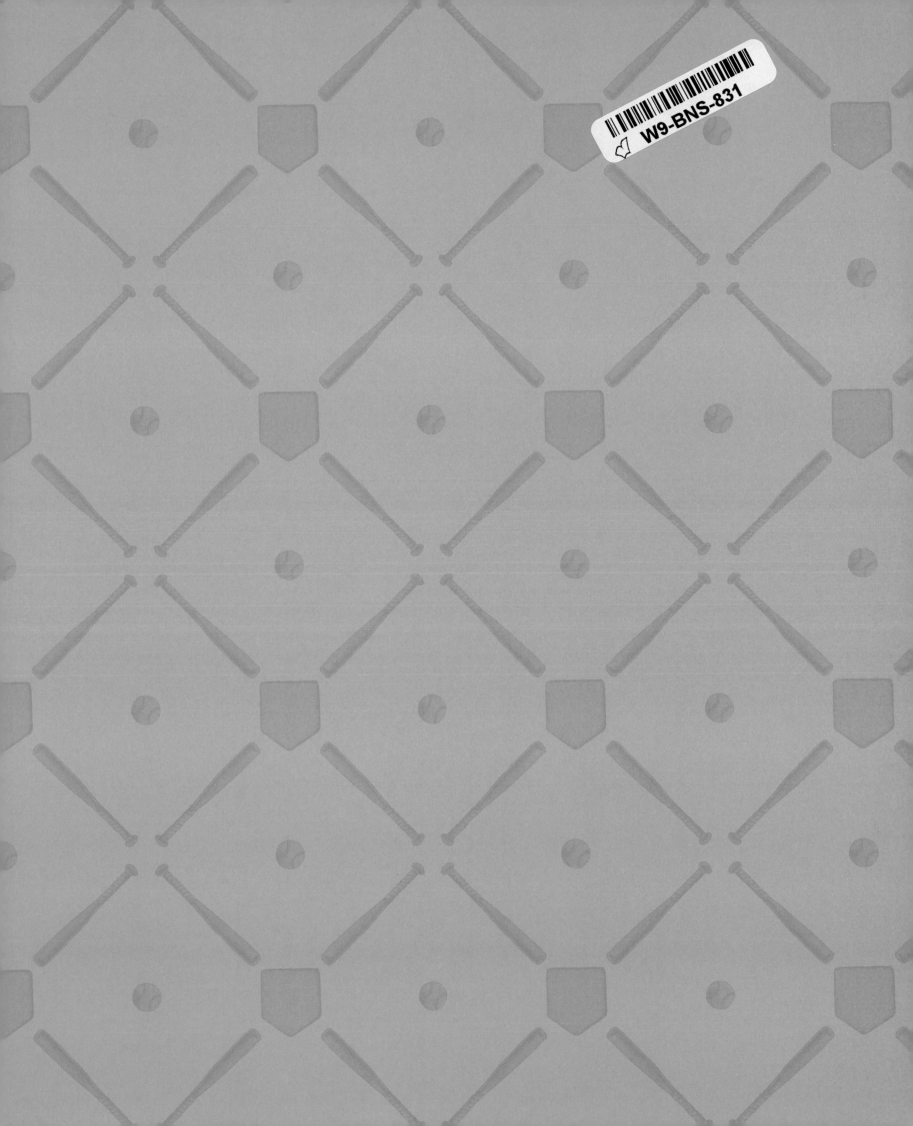

Little Teammate

Alan Williams
illustrated by Stephen Marchesi

NEW YORK

NASHVILLE MELBOURNE

Books can only come together with a solid team in place. I've had the privilege of working with the same teammates for the better part of the last ten years.

Stevie, you're a pro and a lifelong friend. Your willingness to enter into unfamiliar territory with me on this project led to a collaboration marathon that rarely felt like work.

Della, you've seen each book through from idea to press; your expertise shines through each time.

Tara, we started with *Walk-On* and you continue to manage what sometimes feels unmanageable to me.

Thank you **Farm Bureau Insurance** companies for your continued partnership and recognition that Teammates Matter in your communities. Your company culture defines servant leadership.

Stephen, your patience, adaptability, and instinct are unprecedented. You painted *Little Teammate* to endure. I hope our work together has just begun.

Mom, thank you for genuinely caring more about what God was doing in my life than any performance-related outcome.

Whether at the playground, on the court, or in the car, my brothers and I hit each other often during our early years — with or without good reason. **Campbell** and **Bowman**, I'm thankful we've learned to love each other in other ways.

Trammell, **Wynne,** and **George**, this book was inspired by how I want to love you. With age, my strikeouts will become more and more apparent. Your grace I will need.

Amanda, this project could never be meaningful without your engagement in the work. For the timing of your wisdom (knowing when to listen, when to respond), I am grateful. You're my best friend and building a life with you is most special — I love you.

Little Teammate

Text © 2017 by J. Alan Williams
Illustrations © 2017 Stephen Marchesi

Published in New York, New York, by Morgan James Publishing. Morgan James and The Entrepreneurial Publisher are trademarks of Morgan James, LLC.
www.MorganJamesPublishing.com

ISBN 978-1-68350-201-2

Illustrations by:
Stephen Marchesi

Cover and Book Design by:
Stevie Griffin
www.steviegriffin.com

Production Management:
Della R. Mancuso

Printed in Malaysia
10 9 8 7 6 5 4 3

Little Teammate is available at discounts for bulk purchases by corporations, institutions, and other organizations. For more information, please contact:
info@littleteammate.com

Shelfie

A **free** eBook edition is available with the purchase of this print book.

CLEARLY PRINT YOUR NAME ABOVE IN UPPER CASE

Instructions to claim your free eBook edition:
1. Download the Shelfie app for Android or iOS
2. Write your name in **UPPER CASE** above
3. Use the Shelfie app to submit a photo
4. Download your eBook to any device

In an effort to support local communities, raise awareness and funds, Morgan James Publishing donates a percentage of all book sales for the life of each book to Habitat for Humanity Peninsula and Greater Williamsburg.

Get involved today! Visit www.MorganJamesBuilds.com

To my Dad.

A Note to Parents

What do you want your son and daughter to know before they ever play their first game? This was the question I set out to answer as I imagined the Little Teammate character. If you're going to read this to your kids, I really want you to know who inspired this story, and why I dedicated this book to my father.

Before my games as a kid, Dad would leave behind a notecard on my bed with a quote, a Bible verse, and some practical advice.

> *Play hard, be patient, be aggressive, don't worry if you miss a few shots, get your teammates involved, BE READY, DO YOUR BEST, AND HAVE SOME FUN!*

I played college basketball as a walk-on at Wake Forest. Moments before leaving my dorm for our biggest game of the year against North Carolina, there was a knock at the door. It was a courier holding an overnight package. Inside the package was a note from my Dad. Even though he knew my playing time would likely be *zero* this particular night, he had not forgotten. Whether different seasons of my life called me to be a starter or the player sitting farthest away from the coach on the bench, my Dad knew that my brothers and I needed encouragement.

After writing my first book, *Teammates Matter: Fighting for Something Greater than Self*, I traveled to school communities across the United States for almost 10 years. While sharing my story and promoting *team*, I also learned what was happening at various levels of athletics. Continually, I met high school students worn down from feeling as if their lives were one big performance, whereby love from their parents seemed conditional on achievement.

My kids' sports journey has only just begun, so please know that this book is not written from the perspective of the imperfect, unseasoned parent that I am. Rather, the ensuing pages are written by a son who was loved, encouraged, and accepted by also imperfect parents, whether he hit the ball or missed the ball.

Join the conversation at littleteammate.com

Little Teammate steps to the plate.
Just one hit will win this game.

Pitcher nods his head.
Little Teammate remembers
what Daddy always says...

Be ready.
Do your best.
And have some fun.

Cheers get louder.

Pitcher looks taller.

Two strikes already and a runner on third...
Here comes the ball!

Crack! The bat sounds.

Surprise all over Little Teammate's face,
the ball flies over second base.

Chin held high,
CHUG...CHUG...CHUG...
Little Teammate begins to run.

From the dugout, friends begin to yell...
WE WON! WE WON!

After the game,
a **big hug** from Daddy.

I **love** you Little Teammate.
I'm **proud** of you.
It makes me so **happy** to watch you play.

One week later...

Hoping for more of the same,
Little Teammate shows up for the next game.
Here we go again.

Little Teammate steps to the plate.
Just one hit will win this game.

Pitcher nods his head.
Little Teammate remembers
what Daddy always says…

Be ready.
Do your best.
And have some fun.

Cheers get louder.

Pitcher looks taller.

Two strikes already and a runner on third...
Here comes the ball!

Whiff! The bat makes no sound.

Strike three!
You're out!

Chin down low,
Little Teammate looks sad.

After the game,
a **big hug** from Daddy.

I **love** you Little Teammate.
I'm **proud** of you.
It makes me so **happy** to watch you play.

But Daddy...

You've said this before,
when my hit knocked
in the winning score.

Remember what you saw?
Today I missed that ball!

Yes Little Teammate,

but one thing
you must know...

I love you when you **hit** the ball.

I love you when you miss the ball.

I love you just because...

...because you are my Little Teammate.
And nothing can ever change that.

Daddy, I feel so much better!

For the next game I cannot wait...
What should I do when I step to the plate?

That's easy...
Just do the same thing my Daddy told
me when I was a Little Teammate...

Be ready.
Do your best.
And have some fun.

And always know that I'm your **biggest fan.**

Get ready to play baseball.

Helmet
You wear this to protect yourself from the ball when you are hitting.

Bat
You use this to hit the ball. When you get a hit, never throw your bat. Just drop it.

Home Plate
Where you stand to hit a ball and what you touch to score a run for your team.

A Hit
When the bat makes contact with the ball in fair play and you reach a base.

Pitcher
The player who pitches the ball to the catcher behind home plate.

Teammates
The friends on your team. Encourage your teammates whether they *hit the ball* or *miss the ball*.

Umpire
The person who makes sure all of the players follow the rules of baseball.

Strike
1. Swinging at a pitch and missing.
2. Hitting a foul ball with two strikes or less.
3. Taking a pitch in the strike zone.

Pound
Let a teammate know you care about them with a pound.

Can you find all **9** pictures in the book?

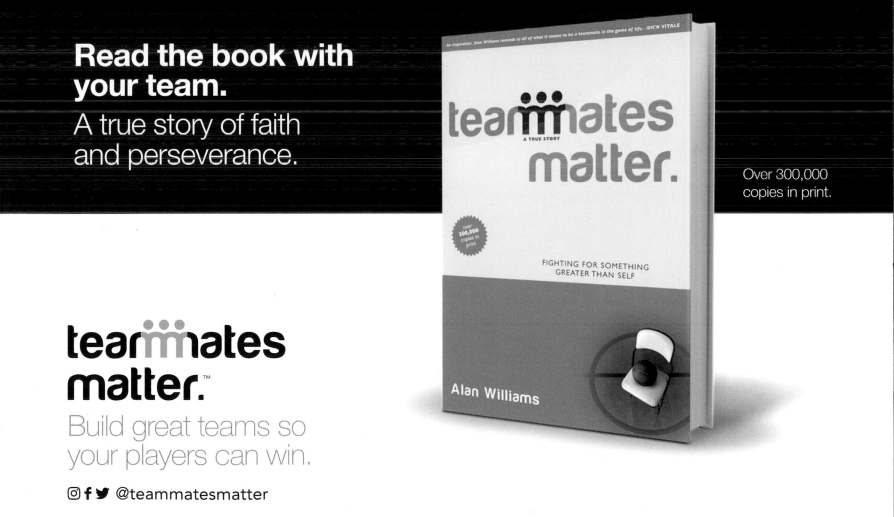